T

TATTOO FOX

A story about a fox who lives
at Edinburgh Castle and loves the
Royal Edinburgh Military Tattoo

by Alasdair Hutton

with illustrations by Stref

Luath Press Limited

EDINBURGH

www.luath.co.uk

For Aline. (AH)

For Granny, and her foxes! (SW)

First published 2013
Reprinted 2014

ISBN: 978-1-908373-93-9

The paper used in this book is recyclable. It is made
from low chlorine pulps produced in a low energy, low emission
manner from renewable forests.

Printed and bound by
CPI Group (UK) Ltd, Croydon, CR0 4YY

Typeset in 11.5 point Din

Text © The Royal Edinburgh Military Tattoo Ltd., 2013
Illustrations © Stephen White, 2013
No text or illustrations from this book may be reproduced without
prior permission from The Royal Edinburgh Military Tattoo Ltd.
All rights reserved.

The Royal Edinburgh Military Tattoo was established for charitable
purposes to support services and artistic charities. In recent years we
have disbursed several million pounds.

Each year we stage a world-class event from which a
substantial amount is Gift Aided to The Royal Edinburgh Military
Tattoo Charities Ltd which is then dispersed as donations to a range
of charitable organisations.

If you enjoy the book then please give a thought to our charitable
purposes and perhaps make a donation, join our Friends or become
a supporter. Find out more at **www.edintattoo.co.uk**

THE ROYAL
EDINBURGH
MILITARY
TATTOO

The Edinburgh Military Tattoo (Charities) Ltd is a company limited by
guarantee Registered in Scotland No. 108857. Charity No. SCO18377.

Patron: HRH The Princess Royal, Princess Anne

Brigadier David Allfrey MBE
Chief Executive and Producer
The Royal Edinburgh Military Tattoo

In July 2011, only a few months after taking up my new appointment, I was on the Esplanade of Edinburgh Castle at 1.15 in the morning watching lighting checks. The dark pools of indigo light were set out like stepping stones towards the Drawbridge. As I watched and listened, I reflected on the step change in my own life and the challenges that might lie ahead.

In the quiet, it was easy to hear a 'patter' of feet on the stairs of the North Stand! When she saw me only a few feet away, the vixen stopped on the bottom step and watched me warily. I held my breath. As the fox recognised that I was no threat, she relaxed, sat on her haunches and continued to watch me. We shared the moment for a short while before she became drawn to some other purpose, licked a front paw and jogged along the front of the Stands, into the Coalyard and away.

I felt privileged to have shared a few moments with a wild creature in the shadow of Edinburgh Castle. I took our meeting as a good omen and speculated that the fox, and her family – perhaps even accompanied by a scarred dog fox – lived in the Castle precincts all year round, making the best of her environment and those things left behind by visitors and the Castle family. I wondered what she and her forebears would have made of our comings and goings. And, I wondered in particular, how she observed the summer invasion of her privacy and the extravaganza of the Tattoo. Would she be the most discerning critic of my endeavours?

Knowing that 2013 was designated 'The Year of Natural Scotland', I made mental note of the encounter and when the time was right asked our Narrator/Storyteller – the eloquent and knowledgeable Alasdair Hutton – whether he might write the story of 'The Tattoo Fox': drawing on the fox's encounters with human beings and our complex world. I asked him to paint an easy picture but set out the story as a gentle morality tale laced with the simple values that might apply to both people and animals. I asked that he might look to thread in the military values of courage, discipline, respect for others, integrity, loyalty and selfless commitment.

Here is his charming tale with beautiful illustrations by Stref – our tribute to the Tattoo Fox.

yours aye

David

August 2013

Contents

Thanks

When Brigadier David Allfrey told me about his encounter with the Tattoo Fox there was a lot of fun in the dark winter nights of 2012 and 2013 thinking about what adventures a fox could have in the Festival City of Edinburgh and at the Royal Edinburgh Military Tattoo.

A number of people have been a wonderful help in turning those rambling thoughts into this little book and all deserve my undying thanks. Any failings in the book are mine alone.

Lindsey Fraser's infectious enthusiasm was tremendously encouraging as her editing skills polished these stories from rough stones to gems.

Stref's drawings are little jewels which remind me of the artistry of Ernest Shepard and they have been beautifully enhanced by Fin Cramb's delicate skill with colours.

As project manager, Nancy Riach in the Royal Edinburgh Military Tattoo office was a terrier, never letting these stories languish; bringing it all together. Also, our wonderful staff, friends and supporters in the Tattoo Office and wider afield, for all their support and encouragement.

Kirsten Graham of Luath was simultaneously patient and dynamic in pushing the project to its successful completion.

Thanks to Morris Heggie from DC Thomson for his wisdom and support.

And I could not have understood anything about the behaviour of the fox without the observant guidance and willing help of the staff of Historic Scotland at Edinburgh Castle.

Finally I have to say the biggest thanks of all to the Fox for inspiring the whole idea.

Alasdair Hutton
Kelso

1

The Long Journey Home

**The homeless fox arrives in town
And soon decides to settle down**

The little fox was exhausted. She dipped in and
out of doorways, shrinking back into the shadows
whenever she heard a noise or sensed trouble.
The summer was over and the moon was clear
in the sky. She had lost count of the days she had
been travelling. Would she ever find somewhere
safe, somewhere she could curl up and sink into a
deep sleep?

On she went, up the narrow road with its tall
buildings on either side. Her eyes were wide and
anxious, watching for danger as her mother had
taught her.

None of the people who stumbled out of restaurants and pubs on Edinburgh's Royal Mile noticed the little fox that September night. Nobody in the queue for the night bus saw her slip across George IV Bridge. Only one person spotted her – a soldier making his way back to his barracks in Edinburgh Castle. He had been visiting his family for the weekend.

"I have never seen a fox with white socks before," he said to himself. "What a beautiful animal."

Realising that she had been seen, the little fox backed into a doorway, terrified. The soldier crouched, holding out the end of the ham sandwich his mother had made for his train journey. But despite the ache in her stomach the fox did not dare take it from his hand. So he threw it gently towards her.

"Take it! Go on..." The soldier backed away. He could tell the fox was hungry. She was thin. And frightened.

The sandwich lay on the pavement.

The fox's mouth watered.

"It's for you," said the soldier quietly. "You look as
if you could do with a decent dinner."

The temptation was too much. In a single movement
she snatched up the sandwich and ran as far and as
fast as her weary legs could carry her. She risked
looking back only once. The soldier was smiling as
he watched her. He meant her no harm.

She dashed round a corner and into a doorway where she devoured the sandwich. It was the first food she had eaten in a long time. She'd had nothing but water from puddles since she'd found a bin that had been blown over by the wind.

After a few minutes the fox plucked up the courage to poke her head out from the shadows. She watched the soldier walking further up the road, towards a huge dark shape.

Edinburgh Castle.

2

A Safe Place?

The little fox is all alone
Is this place safe to make her home?

The fox had not meant to leave the den where she
had been born in the Spring. She and the other
kits had been happy, safe and well fed by their
parents. But something in the late summer air
had tempted her away. Before she knew it she
was alone, in a place she didn't know. At first she
tried to look for her parents, and her brothers and
sisters. Night fell and there was no sign of them,
so she took refuge in a ditch beneath a hedge
and tried to sleep. Her empty stomach woke
her before dawn, so she ate some of the berries
on the hedge and after pouncing on a couple of

sleepy worms she started walking again, keeping to the shadows. The fields and the hedges looked very like the fields and hedges she was used to, but they were not quite the same. As time passed she realised that she was on her own now. She would have to find her own food and make her own den.

So she had left the woods and hills near Kelso in the Scottish Borders where she had been born and headed north. In Lauder she had found the upturned bin full of scraps from a family's Sunday lunch. The left-over chicken bones had been so delicious that she decided to make her home in the garden, beneath a hut. Perhaps there would be more tasty meals. But in the morning a huge cat hissed at her, making it clear that foxes were not welcome there.

On she went, travelling by night if she could. She was too easily seen in daylight. One night, just before dawn she crept in below a feeding trough on a hillside and was quickly asleep, wrapping her tail round her nose to keep warm. But she was not peaceful for long.

 14

The sheep were moving early and woke the sleeping fox. She had just started to creep out of her hiding place when she heard the rumble of a motor and, more worryingly, the sound of dogs running up the hillside. The little fox knew enough to be wary of dogs. It was time to go.

But one of the dogs had spotted her. And it alerted the others.

The little fox plucked up her courage and bounded into a full run, heading for shelter in a small copse of trees.

But the trees were a long way off, and the dogs were trying to drive her away from them. They were gaining on her with every second that passed. She didn't know how much longer she could go on.

All of a sudden the fox heard some piercing whistles and immediately the dogs turned back. Their master had work for them. The fun was over.

Exhausted, the little fox rested in amongst the trees, but it was not easy to sleep soundly when there were dangers all around. She had to keep going until she found somewhere safe.

During the days and nights that followed, she was shouted at by farmers, puzzled by the noise the huge wind turbines made and narrowly avoided being run over by a lorry as she crossed a country road.

But one morning she could see on the horizon the shape of a hill that reminded her of the countryside where she had been born. It looked rather like a big armchair. There was something very reassuring about it. That was where she would settle, she decided.

On she went. She knew where she was going now.

Eventually she reached a huge road – the Edinburgh bypass. She waited in the woodland until night-time when there were fewer cars and lorries and carefully made her way across the four lanes. Once she was safely on the other side she padded silently through the suburbs of the city, past houses and tenements and offices until she came to the hill she had seen – Arthur's Seat.

At last. Somewhere safe with grassy slopes, bushes and rocky ledges.

The little fox was just looking around for a place to make her den when a fierce looking dog fox appeared, chittering at her. Who did she think she was? This was his territory. She would have to move on. She bowed in submission and slunk off. Foxes don't usually attack each other but she was taking no risks.

What was she to do now? There was no choice. The little fox had to move on again.

She ran down the hill and keeping close to the wall round the Palace of Holyroodhouse, she put as much distance as she could between herself and the unfriendly fox. A car screeched by, its siren blaring. Panting, she headed up the narrow road – Edinburgh's Royal Mile.

It was near the top of the Royal Mile that she had been spotted by the soldier on his way back from a weekend away.

* * *

After she had finished the sandwich the little fox sat hunched, looking in the direction the soldier had gone. He had been kind. He hadn't chased her away, or yelled at her, or kicked out at her, as someone had in one of the villages she'd passed through.

Perhaps she could make her home near where he lived? She set off.

After a few hundred metres she found herself at the entrance to a huge arena, full of piles of scaffolding. What a mess! It was hard to know which way to turn. Away in the distance she heard the soldier greet some friends and watched as he disappeared through an archway.

What should she do? She hopped over the piles of poles and skirted round the lorries waiting to take the scaffolding away in the morning until she reached a long wall. The soldier and his friends had gone now. Once again the little fox was on her own. Unsure, she stood and sniffed the air. To her joy she smelled grass, and trees and shrubs. And rabbits.

She skipped through the railings and over the wall and found herself on a steep slope, sheltered by the huge castle above. It was perfect. In a hollow beneath an overhanging rock she nosed into a bed of dried leaves, curled up and fell fast asleep.

3

Friend or Foe?

The fox is hungry and afraid
When the cat comes to her aid

The fox woke as the day brightened over the city of Edinburgh.

From her vantage point on the hillside beneath the castle she could see buses and cars and people. Every so often a plane would fly across the sky. It was all so different from the fields and woodlands where she had been born. She stretched as best she could, reluctant to leave the safety of her new den. But soon her stomach began growling. She needed something to eat.

Rabbits! Her mother had often brought the kits rabbits to eat and she had tried to teach them to hunt them. The fox ventured out into the autumn morning and looked around the hillside. There wasn't a rabbit to be seen anywhere. She would have to think again.

"Looking for something?"

The fox jumped and swung round.

"I said... are you looking for something?"

The voice was coming from above her.

The fox squinted up towards the wall where she saw an enormous grey cat, the end of its tail twitching slightly.

"I am looking... for something to eat," replied the fox. She steadied herself and got ready to run. The only cats she'd ever met had chased her away.

"Rabbits?" suggested the cat. He seemed pleasant enough.

"That would be perfect," said the fox politely. Her mouth was watering at the thought.

"Good," said the cat, "but you'll have to cross the Esplanade and try the other side of the Castle. There are hundreds of the blighters there."

"Oh..." For a moment the fox wondered if this was a trap.

"I'm the Edinburgh Castle Cat, by the way. Who are you? Are you passing through? Or planning to stay for a while?"

'I'm a fox from the Borders,' said the fox, 'and I'd love to stay. I've been travelling for days, and need to make a den for myself.'

"Well you couldn't have chosen a finer residence," said the cat. "City centre with lovely views and lots of food scraps. I live up there in David's Tower. It's part of Edinburgh Castle. I'm delighted you'll be my new neighbour."

"I'll share my rabbits with you," offered the fox. "If I ever manage to catch one."

"Oh don't worry about that! I catch the odd mouse, just to earn my keep, but mostly I'm fed by the regiment. I'm their unofficial lucky mascot so they like to keep me happy. In fact, I'm a bit on the tubby side at the moment," he said, looking down at his rather large furry tummy. "It's always the same at the end of the tourist season. So many tempting snacks around the place. Perhaps you'd like to share a little of my food?"

The fox didn't know what to say except, "Thank you..."

The cat explained that he was given one very large meal every day at lunchtime. "You'll hear a loud BOOM!" he said. "That's the One O'Clock Gun. It makes a frightful noise, but they're not shooting anybody. In the past it was to help the sailors down in the docks at Leith set their clocks accurately. Nowadays the people of Edinburgh depend on it so that they aren't late back from their lunch breaks.

Anyway, once the BOOM! is done and dusted, slip through the tunnel just by the entrance to the castle and follow the cobbles round until you reach the Tearoom – you'll know it by the delicious smell of the cakes. Run round the back and I'll be waiting for you."

"Thank you very much," said the fox again.

"You're most welcome. Once the Tattoo's finished, things become a little dull around here. I'm glad to have some company," said the cat. He stood up, swishing his tail. "See you just after one o'clock," he said and made his way along the wall back towards the castle.

The fox couldn't believe her luck. A cat who was friendly, and who was happy to share his food! She wanted to hunt for her own food, of course, but it was good to know that she didn't have to, at least while she settled in to her new home.

She decided to explore. She dug up some worms and bugs, and even caught a mouse. There was no reason to venture far from her new home that morning. She was still tired after the long journey, and rather nervous. Time seemed to pass slowly as she waited for the BOOM!

But when the BOOM! came, it was louder than the little fox could possibly have imagined. She leapt to her feet and vanished behind one of the bushes. Her fur bristled with fear. What was that? A few moments passed before she remembered. The Castle Cat had warned her about the One O'Clock Gun. There was so much she would have to get used to in her new home. But first things first. Now it must be time for a meal.

Swiftly and as inconspicuously as possible, she slunk over the wall and ran along the shadows until she reached the tunnel. It was just as the Castle Cat had promised. She dashed onwards. The thought of food was wildly exciting.

And so was meeting up with her new friend once again. There were so many things she wanted to ask him.

But one question niggled away at her more than all the others.

What was the Tattoo that the Castle Cat had mentioned?

4

The Riding of the Marches

When a badge has gone astray
The fox is there to save the day

The fox had been living on the hill beneath Edinburgh Castle for a few days and she was settling in well. The Castle Cat had been most helpful, showing her around and pointing out the best places to catch mice. She had tried hunting rabbits a number of times, but they always seemed to be one step ahead of her.

One morning the fox was explaining about her latest failed attempt at hunting when suddenly the Castle Cat stood up, his tail twitching madly.

"Oh dear. It's that time again. They're on their way," he said. "I don't much like crowds. I'm not sticking around for this!" And without further ado, he strutted off, back to his home in David's Tower.

What was his problem? The fox pricked up her black-tipped ears. What was that? She picked up the sound of a great many horses. They were a long way off but she had hardly seen any horses since she left the Borders and wondered why so many would be gathering in a city like Edinburgh.

The canny fox was curious, and as the Castle Cat had gone home she decided to find out what was going on. She picked her way carefully to a secluded spot where she could see down the Royal Mile. Dozens and dozens of horses were slowly making their way up the street in her direction. Perhaps they had come from the Palace of Holyroodhouse where the Queen lived when she visited Edinburgh.

"I wonder if I will see the Queen," thought the fox. But the horses were not pulling a carriage. Surely the Queen would not travel without a carriage. The sound of music was becoming louder and louder. The fox looked more closely. First came rows of pipers and drummers leading hundreds of horses. Their riders were carrying flags and banners and wearing sashes in every sort of colour, each one indicating the town they came from. They looked very smart and a large crowd of people had lined the street to cheer them as they came up the hill.

The fox ran through a network of alleys and holes which brought her out close to the Mercat Cross next to St Giles Cathedral. Important looking people had assembled at the old Cross, where all the Royal Proclamations and other important announcements are made. They were being guarded by well dressed, respectable looking men in black coats carrying silver truncheons.

The pipers and drummers came to a halt, followed by the horses. It was quite a crush. No wonder the Castle Cat had left her to it. The little fox scuttled off to a safe viewpoint.

None of the riders noticed her peering through the railings but she managed to catch the eye of one of the horses. "What is going on?" she whispered. "Is this the Tattoo?"

"Don't be daft. Don't you know?" said the horse rather superciliously. "This is the Riding of the Edinburgh Marches. This is one of the many festivals we celebrate in Edinburgh. Surely you know that Edinburgh is a Festival City?" He tossed his head.

The Marches! How could she have forgotten?
Immediately the fox knew why she recognised
the banners and the sashes and the rosettes.
She was a Border fox and she had seen hundreds
of horsemen like this riding the marches of the
Border towns when she was a kit.

"And who is that man wearing the robes and
the chain, the one who's speaking?" she asked
quietly.

"That, my dear fox," said the horse, "is the Lord Provost of the City of Edinburgh. He is a very important man."

"And who are those other important looking men with their silver sticks?"

"Those are the Lord Provost's bodyguard, the High Constables of Edinburgh," replied the horse. He sounded rather irritated with all her questions and tossed his head again.

The fox wanted to ask more but the horse obviously thought he was much too important to talk to a fox.

The riders had returned to their mounts now that the speeches were finished.

The horses shuffled about as their riders climbed onto their saddles once again. Then they set off up the Royal Mile towards Edinburgh Castle. Some of the horses snickered and stamped, nervous of such a crowd in a place many miles from their stables and paddocks. In all the confusion of riders mounting and horses moving the fox noticed that one of the riders, a young man who was wearing a blue and white sash, had dropped his rosette. It was a beautiful circle of colours with many coloured ribbons dangling from it. What caught the fox's eye was the handsome silver badge in the middle.

In the scuffle one of the horse's hooves had kicked it through the railings into the nook where the fox was hiding.

The fox looked at the rosette. That young rider would miss such a precious looking object, she decided. She could leave it lying there – that was the safest option. But the fox knew that wasn't the right thing to do. So she took it carefully in her mouth and dashed back through her maze of alleys to the Castle Rock. She peered over the side into the road below, where the horses were being loaded back into their horseboxes, ready to go home.

The fox looked down and recognised the young man who had dropped the rosette. He had realised it was missing by now, and he and his friends were looking for it.

"Come on!" called one of the horsebox drivers. "We can't wait all day! That rosette will have been trampled and ruined by now. You should have been more careful."

The fox could see that the young man was sad to have lost his rosette. It had been specially made for him in his town's colours, with the silver town badge in the middle and all the ribbons from his previous rides fluttering from it.

There were still a lot of people about but the fox was quick. She dashed down the steep slope of the Castle Rock and dropped the rosette by the edge of the pavement where the riders might see it. Then she sprinted back, hoping she hadn't been spotted.

But she had.

"A fox! A fox!" shouted a boy who was helping load up the horses. "I saw a fox drop something!" He jumped up and down and pointed at the pavement and the young man sprinted up and recovered his precious rosette.

"Honestly – it was a fox. She had your rosette in her mouth!" Excitedly the boy told everybody what he had seen.

"Foxes are thieves," said the driver gruffly. "You won't find a fox returning lost property."

But the young man ruffled the boy's hair and said quietly, "I believe you." Then he turned and called in the direction the boy was pointing. "Thank you, fox. This is the best present you could have given me!" He proudly pinned his precious rosette back on his jacket.

By now the fox had made sure that she was well hidden again. She was glad that she had taken such a risk but she would be more careful in future. She watched as the last of the horses were led into their horseboxes and driven away.

Later that evening the fox told the Castle Cat what she had seen.

"I'm delighted that you had such a splendid time," he said. "But all those hooves..." His tail twitched anxiously. "That's one of Edinburgh's festivals about which I'm not quite so enthusiastic."

"I thought it might have been the Tattoo," the fox said.

"No, my friend. That's the Riding of the Marches. It takes place every year so that the people of Edinburgh know that their common lands are well looked after. You'll have to wait a while until the Tattoo."

5

A Lost Child

A little girl is lost and sad
The fox knows how to make her glad

The autumn was turning to winter, and by now the fox was very much at home around Edinburgh Castle. She could barely remember what the Scottish Borders looked like.

Every night she would return to her den in the rocks beneath the castle, but during the day – when she wasn't hunting rabbits – she spent her time in the castle grounds, much of it with the Castle Cat. By now she was becoming quite a good hunter, so she didn't need to eat the Castle Cat's leftovers. Sometimes she was even able to offer some of her dinner to the Castle Cat. He was most appreciative.

On bright days the fox loved to snuggle into the shrubs and enjoy the winter sunshine. Tourists came to visit St Margaret's Chapel before walking round into Crown Square to visit the War Memorial. They would take a tour of the Scottish Crown Jewels and look into the bedroom where King James, the king who united the crowns of Scotland and England in 1603, had been born. They never realised that there was a fox only a few metres away.

Her favourite place was in the low bushes behind the Scottish National War Memorial right up at the very top of Edinburgh Castle. She liked it there because it was so high up, and the views north towards Fife and south towards the Pentland Hills were beautiful.

She also liked it because people tended to be quite calm when they visited the Memorial. The Castle Cat had explained that the large building was built by a very sad country to remember all the Scots who had died in the First World War. Many of the visitors opened the huge books lying in the Memorial, looking for the names of people from their families. They were often thoughtful and quiet as they walked around the area.

43

That morning, as she made her way up the Castle Rock from her den, the little fox could see the soldiers guarding the Castle, the sentries, marching up and down in their smartest uniforms.

"Something important must be happening," the fox thought. Perhaps it was the Tattoo? She still didn't really know what the Tattoo was. All the Castle Cat would say was that she'd know it when she saw it.

Most of the soldiers and the sentries knew the fox by now. When they saw her coming in the morning they would usually finish their marching and do a quick practice salute with their rifles as she walked sedately past them over the drawbridge. They would laugh as she ran past startled visitors to the Castle, up the cobbled hill, below the portcullis and up the Lang Stairs. That was the shortcut to her favourite spot.

But today there was no time for laughter. The soldiers didn't notice her at all.

When she reached the top of the stairs it was only a short dash to the shrubs behind the tall windows of the Memorial building.

Once safely there, the fox did not doze as she sometimes did, for she could sense a buzz of excitement among the visitors and saw that the stewards were gently clearing them back from the middle of the road up into the Castle. She looked to see if the Castle Cat was around – he was usually able to tell her what was going on. But he was nowhere to be seen. So the little fox ran across to the wall so that she could peep through one of the mock gun ports.

Suddenly in a rush, three vehicles hurried up the hill. Sitting in the middle one the fox recognised the Queen's daughter, Princess Anne. So that was what was happening! Princess Anne often came to meetings in the Castle. She was always smart and looked happy as she waved to the crowd. The visitors had not realised she was coming so they were especially delighted to see her.

Then after the cars had passed by, the fox heard a young American woman say to her husband, "Where's Aline?"

"Isn't she with you?" He was pushing an empty buggy.

"No… I thought she was with you!"

The fox could tell that the mum and dad were very worried. They both started calling the little girl's name again and again.

The fox remembered how miserable she felt when she lost her mother and father and brothers

and sisters. Slipping out of her hiding place
she listened especially carefully, for foxes have
much better hearing than people. Eventually she
heard something. She was certain it was the faint
cries of a child. But the mother and father were
heading in the wrong direction!

The fox was sure that the sound was coming from
behind the Great Barracks so she took off as fast
as she could, running along walls and through
shadows and squeezing through a locked gate.
She knew it was risky and that she was in danger
of being seen, but that didn't matter as much as
finding the lost child.

At last she came round a corner where she saw a
very pretty little girl with curly blond hair and blue
eyes sitting on some steps. She was crying and
obviously completely lost. This must be Aline.

What could she do? The fox couldn't pick up Aline
as she had picked up the dropped rosette!

The fox thought for a moment and then dashed back to where she thought she might be able to find Nick, one of the Historic Scotland stewards she particularly liked. He often saved her some crusts from his sandwiches. There he was! He had just finished one of his tours.

Catching his eye, she ran round and round and then dashed towards the back of the barracks where members of the public do not usually go.

48

"Well, I never," thought Nick, "I think that fox is trying to tell me something." He had to run to keep up with her.

Sure enough, the steward found the little girl sitting on the steps and as he comforted her he reported on his radio that the lost child was safe. "I'll bring her to the café," he said. "Out!"

"Let's follow that lovely fox," said Nick to the little girl. He had worked at Edinburgh Castle for many years and had lots of experience of returning lost children to their anxious parents. "She's a very special fox. I love her black-tipped ears, don't you?"

After a little while, Aline stopped cying. She took Nick's hand and together they followed the fox back to where her parents were waiting. As soon as she was absolutely sure the little girl was safe, the fox ran off round the back of the café.

A few moments later she was safely in the arms of her father.

Nick explained that the little girl had actually been found by a fox. "She's part of the Historic Scotland team here," he said, smiling.

"Fox!" said Aline, nodding and pointing in the direction in which the fox had disappeared.

"I would like to hug that fox," her mother said.

"Nice idea," said Nick, "but please don't. She is friendly but she is still a wild animal."

"We had better take this little one home," Aline's father said. He shook Nick's hand. "Thank you for your help. Just wait till I get back to America and tell all our friends what clever foxes you have in Scotland!"

6

Christmas Eve

On Christmas Eve the fox can speak
And leaves a thief without a squeak

There is an old legend that on Christmas Eve
people can hear what animals say from midnight
until the dawn. All the animals know it's true but
very few people do.

"It's nearly Christmas," said the Castle Cat one
day. "How would you like a bit of a treat?"

The fox had not heard of the legend, but once her friend had told her about it she could not wait until midnight on Christmas Eve to go down to the city and have some fun with the people there. She hoped it wouldn't snow. The Castle Cat had made it quite clear that he wouldn't be going anywhere if it snowed. "Can't stand the stuff!"

Luckily for the fox this was not going to be a white Christmas. The two friends set off down the Castle Rock and across Princes Street Gardens.

Everybody was very jolly that evening. They were on holiday from work and school, and there were lots of parties to celebrate Christmas.

First the fox and the Castle Cat sat just inside the railings of the Gardens alongside Princes Street and every time someone passed they would call out "Happy Christmas!" They loved watching the startled looks on the faces of the people who could hear the two voices but see no-one near them.

When they were tired of that game they dashed across Princes Street to where they could hear people singing Christmas carols. They were being accompanied by a brass band which made the fox a little nervous, but the Castle Cat reassured her. "I love the sound of a brass band," he enthused. "Just listen to the wonderful harmonies and rhythms. There's nothing like it!" In Rose Street they found a lot of people enjoying themselves, singing and yelling Christmas greetings at everybody who went past. There was music blasting out of all the pubs and restaurants.

"Is this the Tattoo?" asked the fox.

"No!" said the Castle Cat. "This is very definitely
not the Tattoo. Don't worry – you'll know it
when you see it. Now come along – we've some
spooking to do!"

They waited in the shadows beneath one of the
shop windows as four men made their way along
the road towards them, laughing and singing.

"Behind you!" the fox piped up mischievously.
Immediately all four men turned round and round
in circles.

"Did you say that?" one of the men said, poking
his friend in the arm.

"No!" the friend shouted.

"It must have been that fox," one of the others said. He peered over at where the fox and the Castle Cat sat, not moving a muscle. "Yes... A talking fox. That is amazing. I am going to catch him and put him in Edinburgh Zoo," he said, and took a wild lunge in the animals' direction.

"Come here, you devils," he shouted. The other men just laughed.

The fox and the cat decided to make themselves scarce and trotted away down a dark lane. Just as they turned the corner they saw two men. The first looked as if he had been at a party. The other man looked less smart. Suddenly the other man knocked the first man to the ground and started going through his pockets.

"What...? Help!" cried the man, trying to fend off his attacker, but there was nobody else about.

"I do not like the look of this," said the fox. "Stop!" she shouted.

The thief looked up, blinked, shook his head and went back to rifling the other man's pockets.

"Don't move..." he muttered.

There must be something they could do.

"Go and get help," the fox told the Castle Cat, "and I will keep this thief here." She wasn't sure how she was going to do it, but she was determined that the thief wouldn't get away with it.

The cat raced off and soon found two policemen walking slowly up Rose Street exchanging jokes with the Christmas revellers.

"Quick," said the cat, jumping about in front of them. "There is a man being robbed, just round the corner in one of the lanes."

The two policemen looked at the cat in astonishment. "A talking cat? I do not believe it."

The cat did not have time for explanations.
"Please, hurry or he will get away," he urged and
set off towards the lane.

The two policemen shrugged and followed the cat
out of curiosity. They could not quite believe what
they had seen. Or heard.

"There are some strange things going on this
evening," one said to the other as they jogged
after the cat.

Nothing could have been stranger than the scene that met them when they came round the corner. A fox had the thief's trouser leg in her teeth. He was trying to beat her off but she was too nimble for him and just as he thought he had shaken her off, she tripped him up and he fell to the ground.

"Help! Help!" The robbed man's cries were growing more and more desperate. Now that they realised that there really was a crime in progress, the two policemen snapped straight into action. They ran as fast as they could and grabbed the thief. One of them clipped a set of handcuffs round his wrists. Immediately she was sure they had him, the fox let go and skipped out of range.

The other policeman was taking care of the victim. "We're just off Rose Street." Puffing and panting, he spoke into his radio. "You had better send an ambulance to the South Lane. One adult male with head injuries. I do not know how badly hurt he is. He is certainly very woozy but I think he'll be fine. And send a van as well. We have his attacker."

The fox and the cat slipped back into the shadows to watch and soon an ambulance and a police van arrived. The paramedics dashed out to help, and two more policemen jumped out of the van. Before long both men were taken away, one to the hospital and the other to the police station.

The two policemen, their job done, turned round in circles, scratching their heads.

"I'm sure it was a cat who alerted us to this crime," said the first one.

"You're absolutely right," said the other. "Sounds daft, but it's true."

The first policeman stopped for a moment, as if he was thinking. Then he said, loudly, "I do not know how you did it. But thanks."

Both men waited for a moment. "Did I just hear 'You're welcome'?" the second policeman asked, astonished.

His colleague nodded. "That's exactly what you heard," he said. He rubbed his forehead. "What a strange Christmas Eve."

As the two men walked away, the fox and the cat heard one of them saying to the other, "A talking cat and a strong-arm fox. How are we going explain that in the report to the Chief Inspector?"

The Castle Cat purred in satisfaction. "We make a good team," he said to the fox. "But I'm exhausted."

They decided that they'd had enough fun for one night. It was time to head for home.

They ran back up the Mound towards the castle and bade each other a good night and a Merry Christmas before they went to their respective beds.

Then they slept like logs until the bells rang out from St Giles Cathedral on Christmas morning.

7

The Hogmanay Fireworks

The fireworks make a lovely sight
But give the Castle Cat a fright.

The fox and the Castle Cat had a wonderful
Christmas. By Boxing Day, they were both rather
rounder, having feasted on the delicious left overs
from the soldiers' Christmas dinners.

Down in Princes Street Gardens crowds enjoyed
the German Market and once it had closed and
everybody had gone home, the fox and the Castle
Cat ran down to finish off *their* left overs too.

One evening they took a shortcut back to the
Castle Rock but found that they were walking
across an ice rink. They never did that again.

Although it was the Christmas holiday, there was lots going on in and around Edinburgh Castle. Lorries drove up and delivered huge boxes of equipment. A special team of men and women were hard at work, preparing the Castle for the Hogmanay Firework Display.

"Is this the Tattoo?" asked the little fox.

"Not yet," said the Castle Cat. "You must be patient."

"What are the Hogmanay Fireworks then?" asked the fox. Sometimes she thought she would never find out what the Tattoo was.

"Well," said the Castle Cat, "think of the One O'Clock Gun, and multiply it many times over. But even louder."

The fox tried to imagine how loud that might be.

"Then add lots of lights, fired high up into the sky. And lots of squealing and popping too."

The fox could not decide whether she liked the idea of the Hogmanay fireworks or not.

"Oh, and there's music too. Lots of bands play in the bandstand in Princes Street Gardens. It's a big party," the Castle Cat explained. "Stick with me and you'll be fine," he reassured her.

The men and women continued to work in the Castle, laying long cables and fixing boxes and bags along the ramparts. There was lots of shouting as they checked their instruction sheets and made sure everything was exactly where it was supposed to be. They kept crossing their fingers for good weather. "We don't want to have to cancel the fireworks this year."

The fox disliked the smell from the boxes and bags and she stayed close to her den. The Castle Cat visited occasionally. He was very relaxed about all the activity.

"Happens every year," he told the fox. "Ten minutes of mayhem, and it'll all be over. Hey presto – it's the New Year!" He promised to come and collect her so that they could watch it together. "It really is spectacular. Once you get used to the noise you're going to love it."

It was late on Hogmanay when the Castle Cat made his way down the rock to the fox's den. They could hear music far below in Princes Street Gardens on the other side of the railway line. They could see from the clock on the Balmoral Hotel that the Hogmanay Firework Display must be about to start, so they decided to make their way further down the rock to watch.

All of a sudden they heard thousands of people yell "Happy New Year!" and with a swooping squealing noise, and lots of bangs, the firework display began.

The fox did not know what to think. Normally she avoided loud noises – they made her nervous. But there were so many bangs and crashes that there was nothing she could do now. And then there were the fireworks themselves. The fox had never seen anything like it.

Bright lights shot into the air, creating even brighter lights of every colour to shoot even further up into the air, making huge flowers of fire in the sky. One after the other, time after time. The crowds ooh-ed and aah-ed, their screams of delight adding to the noise.

Then suddenly, without any warning, a great waterfall of white light came pouring down the Castle walls, cascading over the rocks. Sparks flew everywhere.

And they were coming their way.

Before they knew what was happening the two
animals were showered by the fiery light. The fox
jumped out of the way of the sparking flames,
but the Castle Cat was not as quick. Some of the
sparks landed on his back and his fur began to
smoulder. The fox watched, horrified as her friend
started to run down the rock, miaowing with
fright, his thick fur on fire.

Without a thought for her own safety, the fox
immediately set off after her terrified friend.
As soon as she got close enough she leapt on to
the Castle Cat's back and rolled him over and over
down the hill until the fire on his back was out.
The grass was quite wet so it did not take long.

When the two animals finally came to rest they
lay in complete silence while the fireworks
continued to rage overhead.

Finally the noise was over, and the crowds began to make their way home.

It was the Castle Cat who spoke first. His voice was a little wobbly. "You saved my life. I am so lucky to have such a loyal and brave friend. How can I ever thank you?"

"I did what I had to do," replied the fox quietly. She was so relieved to find that her friend was safe and sound, apart from some singed fur. "Let's go home."

Slowly the fox and the cat made their way up through the woods towards Edinburgh Castle. When they reached the fox's den she turned to the Castle Cat and said, "I'm glad that wasn't the Tattoo."

"So am I," he replied. "I much prefer the Tattoo." And he padded off into the darkness.

8

Captured!

**The fox is given quite a shock
She's caught and taken off the Rock**

It was a few weeks after the Hogmanay Firework Display and the fox was lying in her favourite spot behind the Scottish National War Memorial. The bushes sheltered her from the chilly February wind, but today the sun was shining. It was the kind of day the fox liked best.

Her eyes closed drowsily and she wondered whether she was dreaming – in fact she could swear she could smell roast chicken.

"Mmmm. How lovely it would be to have dinner brought to me instead of having to hunt for it," the fox thought. She had spent a lot of the night before hunting, but she had very little to show for all her hard work.

The delicious aroma lingered on the air. The fox knew that people often dropped bits of food as they walked around Edinburgh Castle. She never went in search of them until the visitors had gone home. But this smell was so tempting that she stirred from the safety of her den in the bushes and went to investigate.

She looked around, her ears ready to pick up the slightest sound, her nose twitching. But there was nobody around. And the only smell was of roast chicken. She padded closer...

So it wasn't a dream. There they were, pieces of chicken nestling in the foliage, just as if they were waiting for her.

She crept forward and started to eat a piece of the chicken meat. Delicious! It was as she stepped nearer for a second piece that she heard a quiet snap. Dropping the chicken and turning her head the fox realised that she had been trapped in a cage.

There was nothing she could do but wait until somebody came to release her.

The Castle Cat strolled by and was astonished to see the fox sitting patiently behind the wire mesh of the cage.

"This is a piece of nonsense," he said crossly.

"Have I done something wrong?" asked the little fox.

The Castle Cat thought for a moment. "It may have something to do with that bin you emptied round by St Margaret's Chapel. You did leave rather a mess," he pointed out. "The stewards like the place to be neat and tidy for the visitors."

The fox hung her head. What would happen to her now?

"Here comes the steward," whispered the Castle Cat. "Don't make any trouble for yourself. I'm sure they'll set you free soon. I'll be waiting..."

The fox looked reproachfully at the steward when he came to check the cage. She wished it had been Nick. He would never have trapped her like this.

"Ah, my beauty, so we have finally got you," the steward said, almost absentmindedly. "Edinburgh Castle's no place for a fox. Don't you worry. We know just the place for you. You will be at home there."

What did he mean? The fox curled up miserably. The idea of living in a place without her friend the Castle Cat was terrible. But one thing was bothering her even more than that. How would she ever find out what the Tattoo was if she wasn't living by Edinburgh Castle any more?

Two men the fox had never seen before placed the cage in the back of a van. They were very careful but she hated every minute of it. They drove through the long tunnel out of the Castle and down Castlehill onto the Lawnmarket.

The fox could not see where they were going but from the sounds and smells drifting in through the van windows she knew they were still in the city. After about 15 minutes, the van came to a stop. The men opened the back door and took the cage out, placing it gently on the ground. The fox's eyes were wide with fear. Why had she been so foolish?

When the cage was opened the frightened little fox bounded out before the men could change their minds.

Keeping low to the ground, she ran well clear of the van, heading over a road and up a steep grassy slope until she felt safe enough to stop. She looked around. It all looked rather familiar. And then she looked up and knew exactly where she was. It was Arthur's Seat – the hill she'd seen while she was making her long journey north all those months ago.

Her heart sank. She had been chased away from here once already and now she was back. At least she knew where the angry fox's territory was so she could avoid that. But there would be lots of other foxes here too, all of them defending their dens. She watched the van drive away. A coach arrived, emptying a lot of people into the car park. Perhaps some of them might drop some food.

But the tourists didn't have time to eat.

"Who'll be first to the top?" called a tall lady in a red jumper, and they all started running up the hill. Hurriedly the little fox made for a thick clump of gorse bushes to rest.

She wriggled as far out of sight as she could. She suddenly felt very tired.

When she woke it took a few minutes to realise that she wasn't in her cosy den in the rocks underneath Edinburgh Castle. And instead of the Castle Cat waking her for a walk round Princes Street Gardens she found herself eyeball to eyeball with a young dog fox. His beautiful tail was standing straight out behind him. His ears were alert, his eyes bright.

Her heart sank even further.

"Oh no. Not again," the fox thought, and said despairingly, "Is this your den? I'm just about to leave..."

"Oh no," said the dog fox. "Please don't. I was just admiring you. I haven't seen you here before. Is this *your* den?"

"No," said the fox. "I live on the rocks under Edinburgh Castle. It is a lovely place and I was very happy there. I made a careless mistake and now they've sent me away."

She laid her head between her paws. "Arthur's Seat is a lovely place to live, but it's not my home," she explained.

The dog fox lay down beside her and she found herself telling him her story, about how she had made the journey from the Scottish Borders, about how she had been chased away from Arthur's Seat, about the soldier who gave her the sandwich, and about the Castle Cat and their adventures. For a moment she wondered about asking whether he knew what the Tattoo was. But she decided against that for now.

"It sounds a splendid place," said the dog fox. "And I'm looking for a new home. Arthur's Seat is rather overcrowded with foxes these days."

The little fox decided that she liked this fox so she said, "Why don't we go and find my den before someone else claims it?"

The dog fox was thrilled by the invitation. They lay hidden in the gorse bushes until night fell and all the visitors had gone.

Then in the frosty evening air, the two foxes set off through Holyrood Park and by way of the little alleys of the Old Town they ran up the hill to the Castle Rock together.

The fox was delighted to be back in her den once more, and she found that there was plenty of room for the dog fox too. At first the Castle Cat was a little jealous. But soon he decided that three could be more fun than two. The trio spent many happy nights roaming the Castle Rock, playing catch in Princes Street Gardens and hide and seek amongst the pillars of the National Gallery of Scotland.

The dog fox turned out to be an excellent hunter, so the little fox knew that she would never need to empty a litter bin looking for food ever again.

9

The Fox Family

The little foxes do not know
That they will see a special show

The two foxes settled down happily in their den
underneath the Castle rock. The dog fox was
a good provider, and they ate well through the
winter, even when there was snow on the ground.

The little fox grew quite plump, and she slept a
great deal, taking leisurely walks through the
daffodils after the Gardens had closed. One day
that spring, the dog fox returned from a hunting
trip to find that two tiny, dark brown, fluffy kits
had been born.

At first they were entirely dependent on their mother for milk and she couldn't leave them alone in the den. It was up to the dog fox to do all the hunting. The Castle Cat showed him all the best spots, and every night he would return to the den with something fresh and delicious for his family to eat.

The kits grew bigger and bigger, and it wasn't long before they were poking their noses inquisitively out from the den, their nostrils twitching at all the wonderful smells. They were a mischievous handful and while their father went out to gather food, their mother was constantly on her guard, keeping them safe and warning them of all the dangers for a fox in the city. When they grew a little bigger she would take them down the rock to explore their surroundings but only after the gates to the park were shut and there were no dogs to alarm them. As they grew older they learned how to hunt for food. Even though foxes will eat what humans leave behind, they much prefer what nature provides.

As the days grew warmer, the foxes often noticed a lady walking up the paths and settling down on a camping stool with her easel and paints. They knew she had noticed them, just as they noticed her. But they all seemed happy to leave each other in peace.

When the kits became less dependent on her for milk, the little fox was glad to escape from time to time. She loved being a mother, but she loved being a wild animal too, free to roam where she pleased, without being seen, staying clear of danger.

One day she was returning from one of her evening patrols. She had caught a couple of mice and was feeling rather pleased with herself. Up ahead she could see the den and her two kits play-fighting in the grass at the entrance. The dog fox was standing guard, cuffing the little foxes gently if they became too obstreperous.

The little fox strolled up the hill towards them, proud of her healthy family with their shiny coats and beautiful tails.

Suddenly, as if from nowhere, a huge dog burst out of the undergrowth. It was heading straight for the den. The fox barked in alarm, and immediately the dog fox bundled the kits into the den, chittering his alarm. He crouched at the entrance, ready to defend himself and his family against the unruly intruder.

Behind her, the fox could hear a man shouting. "Harvey! Get back here! Harvey! Come!" But the dog paid no attention. On he went, rampaging through the daffodils, breaking through the gorse bushes, panting hard, his huge pink tongue hanging out of his mouth. Every so often he would burl round in tight circles, trying to find a lost scent.

The little fox had never run as fast. She had never jumped such distances. Her family was in danger and she had to be there to help the dog fox fend off the attacker. Finally, her heart thumping, she slid into the den, pushed the kits as far back into the darkness as she could and swivelled round to wait.

But where had the big dog gone?

"You're supposed to have dogs under control in these gardens!" A voice below sounded angry. "What sort of dog owner are you?"

The dog's owner did not reply. He was out of breath now, exhausted from chasing Harvey the length and breadth of the steep slope. He bent over, holding his knees, unable to run any further. Every so often he would try to shout for his dog, but he was so breathless that he could hardly make himself heard.

Then suddenly, the foxes heard another voice.

"Here boy... that's my boy... Got him!" It was a lady's voice, calm and steady. It must be the lady who loved to paint.

Harvey's owner made his way over as quickly as he could. "Thank you..." he said as he clipped his dog back on the lead. "He must have smelt something."

"My tuna sandwiches, I think!" The lady laughed. "No harm done."

The man stopped and looked at her painting. "Fox kits playing," he said. "What a beautiful painting."

"They're such handsome animals," said the lady. "And they're living right here in the middle of the city. I keep wondering how they manage. There's so much noise, and so many people. There are the shoppers on Princes Street, the sound of the traffic, the One O'Clock Gun, and the Hogmanay Fireworks, and visitors like Harvey." She stroked the big dog's ears. He was leaning against her now. "But the foxes seem to like it. They're happy and healthy. I've made lots of paintings of them. I might have an exhibition one day."

The fox and the dog fox swished their tails proudly at her words.

"It will be a lovely exhibition," said Harvey's owner. "Thanks for helping to catch my dog. I'm glad he didn't disturb your beautiful foxes."

"If he did, they'll recover," said the lady. "They're very good parents. Very resourceful."

"We took a different route today because there is scaffolding being delivered to the Esplanade," explained Harvey's owner. "I don't know how many truckloads passed us on the way here."

The little fox remembered the scaffolding being taken away, just as she had arrived last September.

"That'll be for the Tattoo," said the lady. "It's that time of year again."

The fox's heart thumped when she heard those words.

So. At last. The Tattoo was on its way.

Whatever that meant.

Once Harvey and his owner had gone and the kits were safe she would go and find the Castle Cat. Perhaps he would finally tell her what the Tattoo was.

91

10

The Fox and the Piper

The fox just loves to be around
To hear her favourite piper's sound

Late spring turned to summer and the foxes watched as the scaffolding on the Esplanade grew bigger and bigger. Men bustled around with wrenches and drills, adding row after row until finally the structure was complete. Soon the seats arrived in huge articulated lorries – nearly 9,000 of them.

At the foot of the Esplanade a large building was created for the control room and for extra special guests. Lorries delivered hundreds of lights and kilometres of cables. Electricians ran around checking connections and sound systems.

The Castle Cat began to explain what would happen during the month of August. "Every single one of these seats will be full every night for three weeks. Whatever the weather. No performance of the Tattoo has *ever* been cancelled. This year's Tattoo will be bigger and better than ever," he told the fox family as he joined them for an evening stroll underneath the huge scaffolding framework on the Esplanade. "I know you want me to tell you what the Tattoo is but trust me, to see it is to believe it. No words could possibly describe it. Just wait and see."

One evening at the very end of July the little fox watched as rows of colourful flags were added all the way round the arena. As the sun set behind Edinburgh Castle she padded silently across the empty Esplanade. She had never seen anything more beautiful. But she still hadn't seen the Tattoo.

The foxes were used to loud noises coming from Edinburgh Castle. The One O'Clock Gun was part of their lives now. But for a few evenings the little fox had heard a new sound, a haunting melody from high up on the castle ramparts. Curious as ever, she decided to find out where it was coming from.

Even though she had heard the BOOM! of the One O'Clock Gun every day (except Sundays) since she had come to live by Edinburgh Castle, the fox had never actually seen the gun being fired. It was time she found out how the BOOM! was made.

So one day, just before one o'clock, she slipped up the side of the Esplanade, wove her way behind the monuments, and ran along the tunnel, which is big enough to let fire engines drive up in case there is a fire in the old buildings on top of the Castle Rock. It seemed a long time since she had run up it for the first time, to join the Castle Cat for lunch.

She knew that she would come out fairly near where the BOOM! came from and made her way swiftly up to a wall which overlooked the road leading up through the Castle. She ran along the top and jumped down behind it. She looked through the little gaps but could not see anything that would make such a loud noise.

So she ran a bit further round and jumping down on to the grass bank saw a crowd of people gathering. Just beyond them stood a big gun pointing over the city towards the waters of the Firth of Forth to the north.

A smartly dressed soldier appeared carrying a heavy, shining tube which she pushed into the back of the gun. Then she stood erect looking at her watch. Waiting. When she was sure the time was right, she reached down, wound the barrel of the gun up so that it pointed to the sky and pulled a handle.

The crowd all jumped and laughed at the BOOM!
of the One O'Clock Gun. Even the fox started,
though she was used to the noise. She was glad
she had found out how the One O'Clock Gun
worked. Now she needed to find out where the
beautiful melodies were coming from. Unnoticed
in all the excitement, she carried on round the
back of the tearoom towards the sheltered grass
of the Western Defences.

A soldier wearing his kilt was walking slowly up and down playing the bagpipes. Every so often he would stop and adjust them slightly before carrying on. He noticed the fox but paid no attention to her. He was entirely absorbed in his music.

The fox sat so enchanted that even when a mouse scurried past she paid no attention to it. So it was the music of the bagpipes that she'd heard in the den! She thought the piper was a wonderful figure, smart, confident, self-contained and handsome. Again and again he would play his tune, determined to be perfect.

Suddenly, out of the corner of her eye the little fox spotted a movement. She turned slightly. Lying on the grass near the piper was a scrumpled up sweetie wrapper. A few seconds later she watched as a small boy fired a second one over the wall. It was clear that he was aiming for the piper but the piper played on, refusing to be distracted.

But when the small boy started calling the piper silly names the fox decided she would teach him a lesson. That clever piper deserved his respect.

She knew the layout of the castle like the back of her paw, so she slipped away. She bounded up through small holes which not even silly boys could manage to crawl through, and came out onto a roof just above the little bully. Gently, she began flicking pieces of moss off the gutter with her paws. The little boy didn't notice at first, but then the mossy missiles became more frequent and a little less gentle, and he stopped shouting insults at the piper and turned to see where they were coming from.

"Mum..." whined the little boy, and pointed towards the fox on the roof. But in seconds the fox hid herself, determined not to be seen.

"Don't be silly, dear. Foxes don't throw things,"
she heard the little boy's mother tell him. "Don't
make things up. Let's go and see the Scottish
Crown Jewels now. Come on..."

The fox heard the naughty little boy wailing as he followed his mother up the cobbled road towards the top of the castle. When she was certain he had gone she returned to the Western Defences. The soldier was packing his pipes away.

One of the stewards wandered by. "Is that you finished for the day, Steven? You're sounding better and better."

"Thanks," said the young piper. "Not long until the Tattoo now. The Lone Piper has to be note perfect."

"And you will be, son," said the steward. "You will be."

The fox ran back to the den. "I know what that beautiful music is," she told the family. "It's the Lone Piper and he'll be playing that tune at the Tattoo!"

She couldn't wait.

11

The Sniffer Dog and the Mobile Phone

The fox has found a missing phone
And melts the police dog's frosty tone

It was two days before the first performance of the Royal Edinburgh Military Tattoo. The foxes knew that the Lone Piper would perform, but that was all they knew. The Castle Cat refused to reveal any secrets – if he knew them. All he would say was, "You won't be disappointed." There was so much activity on the Esplanade that the foxes stayed well away during the day. But late in the evening they would pad underneath the huge scaffolding stands and across the empty parade ground to sit and watch the sun setting in the west. That evening they were joined by the Castle Cat.

"You won't catch me out and about tomorrow," he said. "It's the Sniffer Dogs' first day after their summer break. They'll be completely out of control." He shuddered.

"What's a sniffer dog?" asked one of the kits.

"They're professionals, specially trained, and they have an important job to do – sniffing out trouble and making sure we'll all be safe during the Tattoo – but they can be rather too keen, in my opinion. Every scent is a chance to show off to their handlers. They're frightful show-offs. No manners at all."

The foxes remembered how frightened they had been when the big dog Harvey had almost lumbered into their den. They didn't like the idea of sniffer dogs.

But despite the Castle Cat's warnings, there was something about the Tattoo that drew the little fox back to the Esplanade as soon as the tourists had left that evening. The kits were settled for the night, and the dog fox was happy to stand guard while she bounded back over the wall and under the scaffolding onto the Esplanade.

She stopped in her tracks. The place was not empty. Lots of men and women strode about, talking into radios, pointing here, there and everywhere. Groups of people in different costumes and uniforms gathered by the gates to the Castle and the exit to the Royal Mile. They chattered excitedly in a whole range of different languages. Some practised their dance steps, while others jumped up and down to warm up their muscles.

The fox hid in her favourite spot near the entrance to the Castle. She could see almost everything but nobody could see her.

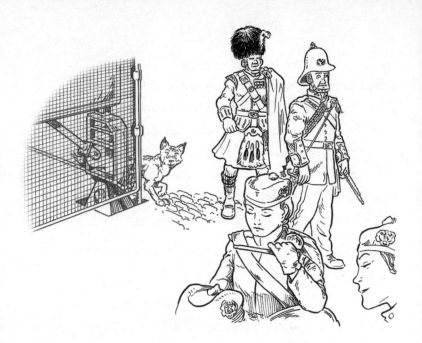

"Dress rehearsal night," said one of the men to a gentleman who was sitting alone in the stands nearby. "There's no going back now!"

"No indeed," said the gentleman. "I can't wait to get started." The gentleman was the Producer of the Royal Edinburgh Military Tattoo. He had been working with his colleagues for the past year to make sure that this year's performance was, as the Castle Cat had insisted, bigger and better than ever. Soon he would find out if all that hard work had paid off.

He spoke into his radio. "Are we ready to go?"

"Sorry, sir. One of the sniffer dogs has gone astray," came the response. "We'll catch the mutt as soon as we can."

"Good luck with that," said the Producer, smiling. He turned and held up his hand, palm out. "Five minutes," he called across to one of his colleagues. "We've got a dog on the loose. I'll alert everybody. It can't have gone far."

Suddenly the fox heard breathing. The fur on her back bristled. There was something behind her. She twisted round and found herself looking into the eyes of what could only be the runaway sniffer dog.

It was very close and she trembled with fright, knowing that she was cornered. She couldn't risk running out onto the Esplanade, but she couldn't see any way to slip past the dog either. She took a step or two back and bared her teeth, ready to defend herself.

The dog looked angrily at the fox.

"What on earth are you doing?" he demanded. "You don't have permission to be here. You must be a security threat." He began to run round and round, his tail beating back and forth. He was very excited. But he didn't look dangerous.

"I was just watching," the fox said carefully. "Who are you?"

"Who am I? I'm an official member of the Tattoo team! I'm doing my job, looking for trouble. Things that shouldn't be here. Things like you! It's a very important job. And you are in my way."

The Castle Cat had certainly been right about the sniffer dog's poor manners. Suddenly there was a sharp shout from one of the police dog handlers, and the sniffer dog began to pant.

"He's pretty bad tempered today," he said. "He's lost his mobile phone and I'm trying to find it for him to keep in his good books. Stay exactly where you are, please, while I search the area." And the dog went off sniffing loudly underneath the rows of seats.

But for once the fox decided not to do as she was told. She didn't like to disobey instructions but these circumstances were exceptional. It was vital that she remained hidden. She took the chance to dash off in the opposite direction.

But as she paused at the bottom of the stand, she caught the Producer's eye. He was the only person on the Esplanade that evening who saw her. He had an eye for detail.

But he wasn't angry. "What a magnificent animal," he said to himself. "I like the idea of a Tattoo Fox."

The fox felt rather small after her telling off from the sniffer dog. She was keen to return to the safety of the den, but she couldn't until all those people – and that sniffer dog – had gone. She found herself slinking further and further into the darkness under the stands. Suddenly she caught sight of a brief red flash of light. Curious as ever, she crawled towards it.

It was a little black box. It flashed red once again. She stared at it.

Suddenly it began to flash and hum and sing a song and the frightened fox scrambled away. When the commotion finally stopped she crept back to have a look. She had no idea what it was but was worried that it might be dangerous. Maybe she could help stop something terrible from happening.

The flashing and humming started again and the fox fairly tore out of her hiding place, almost running into the sniffer dog who came puffing and panting towards her.

"I thought I ordered you to stay where you were!" he barked.

"You did, and I'm sorry I disobeyed you, but come quick," she said. "There is a very strange, flashing, noisy little black box under that stand and it looks dangerous."

"I hope you're not wasting police time," said the sniffer dog crossly.

"I'm almost certain I'm not," replied the fox. She hoped she was right.

"I suppose I had better come. Just to shut you up," said the sniffer dog and he followed the fox into the darkness. Suddenly the flashing and the humming and the terrible singing started again.

"It *is* a mobile phone," said the sniffer dog in surprise. He ran round and round in tight circles for a moment, thinking. "I do not think it is dangerous but we had better be careful. If it is the one my handler lost yesterday you have done me a big favour. Now, make yourself scarce while I go and fetch him."

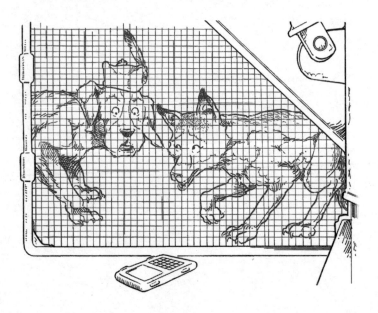

Relieved, the fox slipped out of sight while the dog shot off. He returned moments later with a man in dark blue overalls running at his heels. The man drew out a torch and shone it into the dark recess.

"Good boy," the man said to the sniffer dog. He spoke into his radio. "Can you give my mobile a ring?" Seconds later the phone began to flash and hum and sing.

"Good boy," the man said again and rubbed the dog's head. He crawled on his tummy and stretched as far as he could until finally the mobile phone was safely back in his pocket. Once more he patted the dog's head, then clicked on his lead. "You're sticking with me now," he told him. Then he spoke into the radio. "Stray dog located!"

"Splendid news!" said the Producer and he stood up to give the control room the thumbs up. "Good luck everybody! Let the show begin!"

The sniffer dog turned and winked to the fox in her hiding place. "Thank you for that. You've won me a gold star. You can watch the Tattoo anytime you like. In fact why don't you stay right there? This is the dress rehearsal and that's the best seat in the house!"

12

Welcome to the Royal Edinburgh Military Tattoo

The Tattoo was a brilliant sight
The fox came back there every night

The Castle Cat was right. Nothing could have prepared the fox for what she saw that evening.

She had never seen anything more spectacular or beautiful in her life.

The Tattoo began with the storyteller's voice booming from the Castle and as the show went on he introduced all the different performers.

The little fox watched the entire dress rehearsal without moving a muscle. There were dancers, soldiers marching in different directions, pipers in neat rows, huge military bands, drummers wearing drums that were almost bigger than they were, police dogs who jumped through circles of fire, beautiful horses that danced elegantly, motorcyclists who drove towards each other at high speed and only just missed crashing. There were singers, and competitions to see which group of soldiers could build a gun the fastest. There were people from all over the world, and the fox could tell that they were *all* loving every minute of being part of the Tattoo.

Watching from the stands was the Tattoo team, the men and women who had worked behind the scenes all year. They were so excited to see the results of all their hard work. It was even better than they had hoped it would be.

Her favourite performance of the evening was by the Lone Piper, lit by a single spotlight. It was the young man who had been practising that day on the Western Approaches. His playing was perfect. Everybody stood silently as the beautiful melody rang out from the Half Moon Battery.

And then it was finished. A great cheer rose from everybody on the Esplanade. The Producer was standing applauding them all. "Fine work," he said. "You should be very proud of yourselves!" The Royal Edinburgh Military Tattoo would be better than ever.

The Castle Cat appeared at the fox's shoulder. "Wasn't that the biggest and best evening you've ever had?" he asked.

The fox waved her tail with excitement. "It was. I will come back here to watch every single performance," she said.

As soon as she was sure everybody had gone home, she set off across the empty Esplanade on which she'd watched such extraordinary events only a few hours before.

"There she is. The Tattoo Fox."

The little fox froze. Who was that? How stupid to allow herself to be seen! She had always tried to be so careful.

"Don't worry, Tattoo Fox. I won't hurt you."

The fox looked up into the stands. It was the Producer. He had been sitting writing up his notes now that the dress rehearsal was over.

For a few seconds the fox looked at the man and the man looked at the fox.

"I hope you enjoyed the Tattoo," said the Producer gently. "I hope you'll come back."

The fox waited for a moment, one paw in the air. Then she waved her tail with a mighty swish and disappeared under the stand before loping over the wall and down into the safety of the den.

"We have an invitation to every performance," she told the dog fox. "And I intend to go to them all. After all, I am the Tattoo Fox."

Most nights all four foxes made their way up the hill and over the wall and under the stand to the best seats in the house. Sometimes the sniffer dog would saunter past, but he was busy doing important work, much too busy to worry about chasing them away.

Every night just before the show started a car would drive onto the Esplanade. Often a smartly dressed senior officer of the Army, the Royal Navy or the Royal Air Force would get out. Sometimes it was somebody from the Government, or a member of a foreign royal family, or somebody from the world of sports or the news. The Tattoo's narrator would announce the name of the person, and explain that they would be taking the salute that night. The audience would cheer. The important person would share a Quaich of whisky with the Lone Piper before climbing the stairs to the special gallery facing Edinburgh Castle.

Night after night the foxes watched the show, loving the pipers and drummers in their kilts, frightened and exhilarated in turns by the noise and the speed of the young motorcyclists racing to and fro across the Esplanade, fascinated by the bands and the dancers from far off countries in their colourful costumes, admiring the skill of the marching girls from the other side of the world and the antics of their band, enjoying the precision and grandeur of the marching bands, and the magnificent music of the very smart British Guards bands. Towards the end of some of the performances was a noisy firework display.

Sometimes the little fox went up on to the Half Moon Battery to stand near the Lone Piper while he played. She loved the sound of the bagpipes and the hush that fell over the audience as they listened.

The foxes were always sorry when the last of the bands made their way out of the Esplanade and down the Royal Mile at the end of the night, still playing their hearts out.

After each performance they waited until all the visitors had left, streaming down the Royal Mile talking about the extraordinary spectacle they had enjoyed. Time after time, they heard the words, "I will never forget the Edinburgh Military Tattoo!" and "That was the best show I've ever seen!"

Finally the foxes came out from their secret hideaway and padded across the Esplanade. But the seats were never completely empty.

"Enjoy tonight's show, Tattoo Fox?" the Producer would call. "See you tomorrow."

The foxes would raise their tails as high as they could to show their gratitude.

But the little fox from the Scottish Borders wanted to be more than simply a member of the audience. She made a plan.

"Stay where you are," she told the kits on the very last night of the Tattoo. "I'll be back soon."

She slipped out from under the stands, and waited patiently in the shadows until her moment came. The fireworks went on longer than ever to celebrate the end of a wonderful three weeks of the Royal Edinburgh Military Tattoo. Finally the last of the explosions tumbled from the sky, leaving the bands to march down the hill into the night.

As the Producer watched the pipes and drums marching down the Esplanade and away for the very last time that year, he saw, marching behind them, waving her beautiful tail to the cheering crowd, the Tattoo Fox.

"Bravo, Tattoo Fox," he said to himself, smiling broadly. "I'll see you next year."

THE ROYAL EDINBURGH MILITARY TATTOO

**Year After Year
The Magic Never Fades**

**The Royal Edinburgh Military Tattoo
There's No Show On Earth Like It**

The Tattoo Ticket Sales Office
32-34 Market Street, Edinburgh EH1 1QB
Tel: +44 (0)131 225 1188 **Email:** tickets@edintattoo.co.uk

Or Book Online At:
www.edintattoo.co.uk

THE ROYAL EDINBURGH MILITARY **TATTOO**

In partnership with
✴ RBS

RELIVE THE MAGIC OF THE TATTOO

Live from the Edinburgh Castle Esplanade

This is your chance to relive the stand-out moments from the 65th Edinburgh Tattoo captured live from the Esplanade of Edinburgh Castle.

Experience some of the most unforgettable moments from this summer's spectacular production on CD from August and from October 2014 on DVD.

Available from the Tattoo Shop

The Tattoo Shop
33-34 Market Street, Edinburgh EH1 1QB

Tel: +44 (0)131 225 1188
Email: shop@edintattoo.co.uk

Or Buy Online At:
www.edintattoo.co.uk

DVD £17.95   **CD £13.00**

ALASDAIR HUTTON has enjoyed writing little stories since he was a child. The first Tattoo Fox book was such fun to create that he happily agreed to write some more adventures with the same characters.

He has written and presented the Royal Edinburgh Military Tattoo since 1992 along with hundreds of other tattoos and concerts around the world.

Formerly a journalist and broadcaster, Territorial Army paratrooper, Member of the European Parliament and local councillor, Alasdair is now active in charity work, especially raising money for ex-service men and women.

Alasdair lives in the Scottish border town of Kelso and has two grown-up sons and a grand-daughter who lives far away in America and for whom he loves writing stories.

STEPHEN WHITE lives in Edinburgh and works under the pen-name Stref. He has worked with DC Thomson for many years, producing work for their comic publications, *The Dandy* and *The Beano*. Characters he has drawn include Dennis The Menace, The Bash Street Kids, Minnie The Minx, Billy Whizz, Desperate Dan, Winker Watson, Brassneck, Keyhole Kate, Dreadlock Holmes and many others. He also works on Sunday Post characters Oor Wullie and The Broons. Stephen has had two graphic novels published independently, and a collection of newspaper style cartoon strips, called *Raising Amy*. He is currently working on his forth book, a faithful graphic novel adaptation of J M Barrie's *Peter Pan*, due out in 2015.

The Tattoo Fox Makes New Friends

Alasdair Hutton
With illustrations by Stref
ISBN 9781910021477
PBK £5.99

The fox's friends all gather
round
To watch the greatest
show in town

After discovering
Edinburgh's Military
Tattoo and setting up her
home by Edinburgh Castle,
the Tattoo Fox returns to
her adventures around
Edinburgh. Meeting and
making lots of new friends
along the way (including
the Queen!), the Tattoo Fox
invites them all to her party.

This heart-warming tale was inspired by a real-life encounter
between the Producer of the Royal Edinburgh Military Tattoo
and a fox, late one night on the Castle Esplanade.

> *Hutton is one of Scotland's greatest storytellers* [and] *the
> illustrations by Stref are the icing on the cake.*
> BRIGADIER DAVID ALLFREY MBE

> *Lots of adventures* [and] *the famous Tattoo creates a
> dramatic finale to the story.*
> JENNY BLANCH, Carousel

> *A hit with young readers.*
> EDINBURGH EVENING NEWS

Details of this and other books published by Luath Press
can be found at: **www.luath.co.uk**

Luath Press Limited
committed to publishing well written books worth reading

LUATH PRESS takes its name from Robert Burns, whose little collie Luath (*Gael.*, swift or nimble) tripped up Jean Armour at a wedding and gave him the chance to speak to the woman who was to be his wife and the abiding love of his life. Burns called one of 'The Twa Dogs' Luath after Cuchullin's hunting dog in Ossian's *Fingal*. Luath Press was established in 1981 in the heart of Burns country, and now resides a few steps up the road from Burns' first lodgings on Edinburgh's Royal Mile.

Luath offers you distinctive writing with a hint of unexpected pleasures.

Most bookshops in the UK, the US, Canada, Australia, New Zealand and parts of Europe either carry our books in stock or can order them for you. To order direct from us, please send a £sterling cheque, postal order, international money order or your credit card details (number, address of cardholder and expiry date) to us at the address below. Please add post and packing as follows: UK – £1.00 per delivery address; overseas surface mail – £2.50 per delivery address; overseas airmail – £3.50 for the first book to each delivery address, plus £1.00 for each additional book by airmail to the same address. If your order is a gift, we will happily enclose your card or message at no extra charge.

Luath Press Limited
543/2 Castlehill
The Royal Mile
Edinburgh EH1 2ND
Scotland
Telephone: 0131 225 4326 (24 hours)
Fax: 0131 225 4324
email: sales@luath.co.uk
Website: www.luath.co.uk